D1611906

SCAT! SCAT!

by Sally Francis
illustrated by Linda K. Powell

Platt & Munk, Publishers/New York
A Division of Grosset & Dunlap

Once upon a time there was a little
white cat who had no home. One day she
went walking down the street crying,
"Meow."

By and by she came upon an old woman sweeping the sidewalk. "Meow," said the little white cat.

But when the old woman saw the cat, she said, "Scat! Scat! Go away little cat." The old woman took her broom and swept the cat into the street.

The little cat rolled over and over in the dust.

She picked herself up, shook off the dust, and walked away.

After a while she came upon a man
sprinkling the flowers in his garden.
"Meow," said the little white cat.

But when the man saw a cat in his garden, he turned the hose on her and said, "Scat! Scat! Go away little cat!"

She picked herself up, shook off the water, and walked away.

Suddenly, a big spotted dog came
chasing after her.

"Bowow!" said the dog. "I'll catch you,
cat!"

The little white cat ran and ran until she reached a fence. Then up she jumped. The dog couldn't jump up on the fence, so he barked until he grew tired. Then he lay down and took a nap.

The little cat waited a while. Then she crept very softly along the fence, jumped down, and ran away.

By and by she came to a door. The door
was wide open, so in walked the little
white cat.

But when the woman of the house saw
a cat in her kitchen, she took up a stick and
chased the cat.

"Scat! Scat! Go away little cat!" said the
woman.

And away ran the cat. When she had run a
long way, she saw a window. The window
was open, and on the windowsill was
a flower box.

The little white cat jumped into the flower box and sat among the flowers. The flower box belonged to Amy. When Amy saw the little white cat, she took her in her arms and hugged her. Then she said, "I am going to keep you for my very own cat."

And no one ever again said, "Scat! Scat! Go away little cat."
And the little white cat said, "Purrrrrrr."